Positive African American Plays For Children Book 1

Copyright 2001 NetNia Communications

First Edition

NetNia.Com

Positive African American Plays For Children Book 1

Published by: NetNia Communications

For information, address:
Book Editor,
NetNia Communications
3729 Almazan Drive
Dallas, Texas 75220

Printed in the United States of America
Illustrations by: Emmanuel Gillespie
ISBN: 1-884-163-91-2
Library of Congress Card Number: 2001118101

Disclaimer

This book is designed to provide information about the subject matter covered. It is sold with the understanding that the publisher and authors are not engaged in rendering legal, accounting or other professional services. If legal or other expert assistance is required, the services of a competent professional should be sought.

It is not the purpose of this manual to reprint all the information that is otherwise available to authors and other creative people but to complement, amplify and supplement other texts.

Every effort has been made to make this book as complete and as accurate as possible. However, there may be mistakes both typographical and in content. Therefore, this text should be used only as a general guide and not as the ultimate source of plays for children. Furthermore, this manual contains information on producing an African American children's play only up to the printing date.

The purpose of this book is to educate and entertain. The authors and NetNia Communications shall have neither liability nor responsibility to any person or entity with respect to any loss or damage caused or alleged to be caused directly or indirectly by the information contained in this book.

If you do not wish to be bound by the above, you may return this book to the publisher for a full refund.

This book is dedicated to:

Everyone who is dedicated to the future of our children. If we are to build a beautiful future, we must make a beautiful world TODAY for our children.

"A Good Play Can Create Dreams, Goals, and Inspiration.
Make Sure Our Children Participate!"

Acknowledgements

First, I must give all praises, honor, and thanks to God who touched me with the talents to make it all happen.

Next, I wish to thank our children, Joseph, Zaire, and Zuri, for giving me all the reasons to pursue success, happiness, and prosperity.

I am grateful to my family for their patience, support, and belief during this project. I send an extra special thanks to my husband for his expertise in editing, publishing, and writing abilities. In short, this project would not have been possible without him. Thank you.

To all the wonderful people in my life who has given me encouragement, support, and an ear in time of need, thanks is not a big enough word to say how much I appreciate you all.

Tell Us What You Think!

Tell us what you think about our new product *"Positive African American Plays For Children Book 1".* After you read the plays or stage a performance, send us an email or note. We would love to hear how a big success it was, your comments, suggestions, and ideas for future books. Send correspondence to NetNia Communications:

Email: netnia@netnia.com

Or write:

NetNia Communications
3729 Almazan Drive
Dallas, Texas 75220
214-956-8346

Other Products By The Authors

"Positive African American Plays For Children Book2"(page 113)
"How To Make Black History Month Last All Year"
"Don't Worry Be Nappy-How To Grow Dreadlocks In America And Still Get Everything You Want"

Get online and visit our website at http://www.netnia.com

TABLE OF CONTENTS

Introduction

We had one goal in publishing this wonderful book – to create positive, upbeat children plays that express the culture, history, and pride of African Americans.

If you are planning a children's play or workshop for African American children, you probably had a problem finding a play children will enjoy. ***Positive African American Plays for Children*** gives parents, teachers, counselors, or anyone who works with children, alternative plays that closely identify with the children's surrounding and environment.

This book has five great plays that virtually anyone can direct and produce. The text is large and the sentences are short but powerful. Children will not have any difficulty remembering their lines.

Though there are suggested settings for each play, children or directors can adjust the settings to meet their individual tastes or environment. The plays can be performed at schools, in back yards, churches, boys and girls clubs, or any place where children gather.

There is an entire section of tips and ideas to help you have a great production. As an added bonus, we included copies of programs and tickets at the end of each play. Use them to advertise and market your play.

Positive African American Plays For Children is an excellent tool to help introduce children to theater and drama. Children exercise important skills such as reading, writing, listening, comprehension, and public speaking when they work on a play. They also build high self-esteem and become more confident. Remember, a good play can create dreams, goals, and inspiration. Make sure our children participate.

———Britt Ekland Miller and Jeffery Bradley

Successful Production Tips

"A Good Play Can Create Dreams, Goals, and Inspiration.
Make Sure Our Children Participate!"

This chapter gives you ideas and tips on how to produce an exciting children's play. The basic steps are:
➲ Choose a play.
➲ Assign roles and stage jobs to children.
➲ Decide what type of play to perform: with or without costumes; memorize lines or not; on a real stage or a simple room.
➲ Set rehearsal times and dates.
➲ Create props, sets, programs, or costumes.

➲ Make playbill, flyers, programs, and tickets.
➲ Perform dress rehearsal.
➲ Perform the play.

As the director, you are in charge. Keep in mind, however, that you are not the boss. The success of any play depends on everyone's input. The director listens and tries to use as many of the children's ideas as possible. Helping children understand their characters is probably the most important role of the director.

During rehearsal, everyone work closely together on the scripts, play settings, props, costumes, and everything else needed for a successful play.

The director may require the help of others such as prompters, stagehands, and ushers. A prompter whispers any forgotten lines from offstage to the actors during the actual performance. Stagehands are responsible for stage sets, props, and moving scenery around during performances. Ushers take tickets, seat the audience, and pass out programs. You can use extra kids to perform these task, particularly those that want to participate but do not want to act.

Use the tips below to help you better understand the basic steps listed above. You may not use everything listed below, however, the more you take into consideration, the better your chances of a great play.

TIP #1 Play Script Kit - Before the first meeting or day of rehearsal create a Play Script Kit.

The Play Script Kit contains the script (copied and stapled), the Personal Information Sheet (see tip #2), and the Character Outline (see tip #3). It is recommended that you place all three of these items in folders that have pockets on the inside. As the children receive their folder, have them put their names on the folder and script.

Stress the importance of being responsible and keeping up with their scripts. Set a number limit on how many scripts can be replaced and abide by it.

TIP #2 Personal Information Sheet - Help the children complete the Personal Information Sheet (See page #109)

At the first meeting or rehearsal, have the children fill out the Personal Information Sheet. This form contains the children's name, telephone number, address, and a person to contact. Store this form in a safe place and use it to notify parents of changes in rehearsal times, performances, or sharing important information

TIP #3 Character Outline - Complete the character outline with each actor (See page #107).

To help the children build their characters, have them fill out the Character Outline. The outline gives the children the opportunity to give their ideas, thoughts, or opinions about the life and personality of the chosen character. The children usually have a very good time creating information about their character.

TIP #4 Writing Supplies - Keep plenty of pencil and paper handy.

Pencil and paper will be needed during the production, so make sure you have ample supply for each rehearsal. The children may need to note stage directions, minor changes to the script, or jot down lines they are having problems with.

TIP #5 Stage Space – Have plenty of space for rehearsals and a full production.

Though recommended, it is not necessary to have a stage. Several plays within this book can be produced without a stage. If you choose not to use a stage, use tape or props *(see TIP #9)* to mark any space that will be used for the stage.

The space for the production should be large enough for the cast to make a large circle holding hands. If the space is too small, the actor's full movements will not be seen. If your space is too big, the acoustics will create an unwanted echo when the actors say their lines. Both cases can cause problems with your stage blocking *(see TIP #7)*.

Keep in mind that your chosen space is usually the same place of the performance. Make sure there is enough room to seat your audience.

Tip #6 Stage Areas - Explain the different areas of the stage to the children during the first rehearsal.

The terms used for stage presence are upstage, downstage, and center stage. Upstage is towards the back, farthest from the audience. Downstage is to the front, closest to the audience. Center stage is the middle of the stage. If an actor stands center stage facing the audience, to the right of the actor is stage right, and to the left is stage left. You should use every part of the stage. These terms are used throughout the plays in the book. Try to use these terms so everyone will know exactly where to go onstage.

TIP #7 Blocking - Make sure the children know how and when to move while on stage.

Stage blocking gives the actors direction on where to stand, enter, and exit during the play. Every play in this book contains stage blocking which are in parenthesis before or after each line. Make sure the children do not read or memorize the stage blocking instructions as part of their lines. Keep in mind that important actions should happen downstage closer to the audience. The children should always face the audience when saying their lines.

TIP #8 Lighting – Use lighting to set the moods, place emphasis on action, or change sets.

For example, the stage should be well lit if the setting takes place outside in bright daylight. Or if it's a stormy night, bring the lights down low. You can use a spotlight to direct the audience to a particular action. If you are not using curtains to change sets, simply dim your lights and make the necessary changes to change sets or start a new Act.

TIP #9 Properties (props) – There should be easy access to properties or movable articles in a stage setting.

Props are very important in a stage production. They can be very large and extravagant or very small and simple. In the play " Me In the Mirror," the mirrors that the actors will hold are the props. In the play "The Slick Kidnapper," the chairs are the props.

Props are not always necessary. Actors can act as though they are holding different objects or sitting on chairs and so on. If you have access to the props use them. It is important to have an assistant or stagehand assigned to the props. All props should be labeled with the name of the character and when it will be used during the play.

TIP #10 Costumes – Use costumes to help the audience identify the characters.

Costumes can be rented, borrowed, or you can get parents to make them. They can be simple such as a sign worn around the neck with the character's name on it. This way, actors can switch parts just by changing signs.

You can create costumes with clothes and items from around the house. For plays of historical nature, such as "Back To The Past," you may want to visit bookstores and the library to find pictures that will help you create costumes of the past.

Remember, actors do not have to look exactly like the character to play the part. As long as they can convince the audience that they are the character, it will not matter what they are wearing.

TIP #11 Rehearsal Time - Give yourself and the children plenty of time for consistent rehearsal.

The recommended rehearsal for the plays within this book is 2 hours a day, 2 to 3 times a week. You should be ready for full production in 3 to 4 weeks. Two hours of rehearsal will be the limit for most children before they become distracted and disruptive.

TIP #12 Grouping – Split the children into smaller groups for one-on-one coaching

During rehearsals, separate the children into small groups. The director can go from group to group to give the children individual attention. It also allows the children the opportunity to work together and help each other with their lines. Before ending rehearsal, have the children run through the complete play. This will help everyone work on any problem areas.

TIP #13 Relax and Have Fun - Keep rehearsals upbeat, fun, and exciting with plenty of "sanity" breaks.

The overall objective of a children's play is for everyone to have an enjoyable and unforgettable experience. The director must do all that is possible to make sure rehearsals are positive and upbeat.

Children must feel good about the play as well as themselves. There should be plenty of kind words, smiles, hugs, and laughter during rehearsals.

To help the children relax, take breaks to stretch and perform deep breathing exercises with the children. Not only do they calm down, they also stay focused on the play and their characters.

TIP #14 Dress Rehearsal – Do a dress rehearsal before the performance.

Dress rehearsal is when you bring all the pieces together for the show. Here you make sure everyone knows their lines, setting is correct, costumes fits, props are in place, stage blocking gives sufficient movements, stage has proper lighting, and the playbill created along with the tickets.

TIP #15 Advertise - Use the programs and tickets at the end of each play to advertise your play.

At the end of each play are programs and tickets that can be photocopied or enlarged to make a playbill. Playbills and programs list the name of the actors, the part they play, the director's name, and everyone who helped with the play (costumes, props, scenery, and ushers).

These tips will help stage a very successful production. Remember to take it one day at a time and always remember that you are working with children. When it looks like everything is going wrong, wait and have faith, you will be surprised. When you give your best, they will give theirs. Have a good show and good luck.

Me In The Mirror

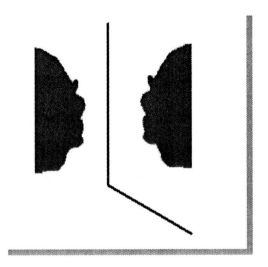

"My nose is too big and flat." "My Lips! Please don't hang lips." " I'm too short!" Ten children go through a metamorphosis from self-hate to self-appreciation and love of themselves regardless of their appearance. Excellent play that builds high self-esteem and a better appreciation of culture.

Recommended age group: 9 - 11

Character Outline

GIRL 1: Believes her nose is too big
GIRL 2: Believes her lips are too big
GIRL 3: Believes her lips are too big
GIRL 4: Hates her hair
GIRL 5: Loves herself
GIRL 6: Believes she is too fat
GIRL 7: Believes her head is too big
BOY 1: Believes he is too tall
BOY 2: Believes he is too short
BOY 3: Believes his feet are big
BOY 4: Believes he is a freak of nature

Time: Present

Props: Hand mirrors

(At Rise: The children enter looking down into handheld mirrors. They slowly walk past one another counting to 15. The audience should not hear the children counting. At the 15th count the children look at the audience and say [very loud] "What's wrong with me?" They look down into their mirrors. They slowly walk to the back of the stage. The children stand very close together in a huddle. GIRL 5 sits in the front of the circle or huddle with a large smile on her face. Children freeze. As they stand, they are looking in different directions. Some children are looking down while others are looking into their mirrors. NOTE: Have children pose in very comfortable positions. They should stand in positions frozen while waiting for their part. GIRL 1 walks forward stops center stage.)

GIRL 1: My nose is too big. My nose is too big and flat. I have to keep a mirror near to make sure that it is not getting bigger. The most freighting thought is that if I am still growing then my nose must still be growing. If this is true, I will soon be able to suck in the world. I want a small dainty nose. I want a nose that is nice and slim, not a lump of clay that sits on my face with two large holes in it. My nose. My nose. (She then covers her nose with both hands. She frantically walks back to her place in the huddle and freezes.)

(BOY 1 raises his head and looks out toward the audience. BOY 1 walks center stage.)

BOY 1: (Stands center stage) I'm tall, too tall.

BOY 2: (Looks at audience) I'm short. I'm short. Can you see me?

(Freezes head down)

BOY 1: (Looks at BOY 2 then turns looking at the audience) I am the tallest person I know. Being tall is good on the court but I don't like to play basketball. I like to read, write and I love math. No one looks at me for the person that I am, they only see how tall I am. I want respect for me, not for how tall I am. (BOY 1 marches back to his position in the back of the stage and freezes.)

(GIRL 2 and GIRL 3 both look up and walk to center stage. As they walk forward, the girls are mumbling softly. GIRL 2 stands center stage right and GIRL 3 stands center stage left.)

GIRL 2 and GIRL 3: (Looking forward.) My lips. My lips. Don't hang. Please don't hang lips.

GIRL 2: (Looking out at the audience) If I had small lips I would never mumble I would always speak clearly. I would stand proud and never let my head hang low. But through some trick of nature I have ended up with big lips. Not just big lips but extra big lips.

GIRL 3: (Turns and looks at GIRL 2) You think your lips are large look at mine. I know that my lips are larger than yours. (Turns and looks at the audience.) If I had small, nice, thin lips, I would wear bright pink lip stick and kiss everyone I meet. I would smile with grace and beauty. (In sadness) I know I have the largest lips in the world.

GIRL 2: (Turns to GIRL 3) No my lips are larger.

GIRL 3: (Turns to GIRL 2) No my lips are larger.

(GIRL 3 and GIRL 4 begin to argue and repeat, "My lips are bigger than yours!" They repeat this 4 times. After the 4th time, BOY 2 moves forward. He walks center stage in the middle of two girls. The girls continue to argue as if he is not present.)

BOY 2: Do you see me? Can anyone see me?

(GIRL 2 and GIRL 3 stop arguing and look at BOY 2. BOY 2 looks out into the audience.)

BOY 2: Nose too flat, lips too big and he (BOY 2 points at BOY 1) has the nerve to complain about being too tall. Can you see me? Move out of my way! (BOY 2 walks over to GIRL 2. She steps back and looks at him.)

GIRL 3: What's wrong with you?

GIRL 2: Yeah, what's wrong with you?

BOY 2: What's wrong with me? Look at me. (GIRL 2 and 3 look at BOY 2)

GIRL 3: And . . .

BOY 2: Can't you see? I'm short!

GIRL 2: My lips are big. I have my problems to think about. (GIRL 2 exits center stage and returns to position and freezes.)

GIRL 3: Me to girl. (GIRL 3 exits center stage and returns to position and freezes.)

BOY 2: (BOY 2 walks back to center stage.) Everyone is always saying, "Isn't he cute?" Or "Oh look at that little boy." Well I'm tired of it. I am _____ (age of actor) years old. I will soon be a man. Everyone is still calling me a cute little (Pause) thing. I'm almost a man! I'm going to grow, and even if I don't grow, I'll show everyone that I'm more than just cute. I'll be the best at whatever I do. I don't even like hearing those words "cute little boy." Can you see me?

(Boy 2 exits off center stage and returns to position and freezes.) (GIRL 4 looks up and puts her hands on her head. GIRL 4 then slowly walks to center stage with hands on her head.)

GIRL 4: Don't look at me. Don't look at me. Go away. Just go away! (Lowers hands) It's my hair, my hair. I put it up it doesn't look right, I try it down and it doesn't look right. I can't do any thing with it. If only I had long and flowing hair, like the women on TV. But my hair won't even move when the wind blows. It would take a tornado to get my hair to move. What can I do? I think I'll cut it, that's the only answer. Yeah, I'll cut it and (dreamy) it will grow again flowing and beautiful.

(GIRL 4 exits center stage with a crazed look in her eyes. GIRL 4 returns to position and freezes.)

(The actors begin pointing and laughing at each other in silence (pantomiming sound and movement). At the count of 10 they stop. Slowly the actors look at their hands, arms, and bodies. They feel their faces and touch their hair. These movements do not have to be done in unison. As one actor is looking at his or her hands, the other actor can be touching his or her face. Silently they count to 5. At the count of 5 they stop, look out into the audience in sadness. Suddenly and in unison they look down.)

GIRL 6: (Looking out into the audience) I'm fat, I know everyone looks at me and they think "Look at that fat little girl or big girl." I want to be thin. (Very loud) I want to be thin!

GIRL 7: (Looking out into the audience) Will you be quiet? I have a head so big that I think it is going to fall off my shoulders and roll down the street. See, I'm going to hold it up maybe that will help.

BOY 3: (Looks out at audience) Help you, what can help me? I have big feet!

BOY 4: (Looks out at audience) I'm a freak of nature, a freak of nature!

EVERYONE: What's wrong with me!

(GIRL 5 stands and walks to center stage. She holds her mirror looking at her reflection. She is humming and singing. She is smiling at her reflection, she is very happy.)

GIRL 5: (Looking into her mirror) Nothing is wrong with me. (Everyone looks at one another in shock.)

BOY 4: (Looking at GIRL 5) You must have something wrong with you.

GIRL 2: (Looking at GIRL 5) You like your eyes?

GIRL 5: (Looking out into the audience) Yeah.

BOY 2: (Looking at GIRL 5) You like everything about yourself?

GIRL 5: I love myself. (Pause. Slowly walks around the stage) Look deep into my mirror. What do you see? (The actors slowly walk forward looking at GIRL 5. They create a semi-circle around GIRL 5. They all freeze while looking at GIRL 5.)

GIRL 5: (Walks to GIRL 1 and holds mirror up to her face. GIRL 5 looks at GIRL 1.) What do you see?

GIRL 1: (Looks into the mirror) I see my mama. She has a nose like mine. (Smiles)

GIRL 5: (Walks to GIRL 3 and holds mirror up to her face. (GIRL 5 looks at GIRL 3) What do you see?

GIRL 3: (Looks into the mirror) I see my grandmother, she has big lips. I love my grandmother. (Smile)

GIRL 5: (GIRL 5 walks over to BOY 2 and stands beside him. She holds mirror up to his face.) What do you see?

BOY 2: (BOY 2 looks deep into the mirror.) My whole family is short. My mother is short. My father is short. Grandma is short. Everyone I love is short. I see all them in me. (Smile)

GIRL 5: (Steps forward to center stage while looking into her mirror.) When I look into my mirror I see pride, dignity and love. (Looks out into the audience) My ancestors fought to survive so that I could be here today. I must be proud. I must always walk with my head held high. I am the future and I will continue to fight, learn, grow and survive. (Looks at the other characters on stage.) We must be proud of our flat noses and big lips. (Pause) What do you see in your mirror?

EVERYONE: (Looking in to his or her mirrors and then at the audience. This line is spoken with pride and is very loud.) I see beautiful, beautiful black me. What's wrong with me? Nothing's wrong with me!

(The cast exits stage left in a line. They enter from stage left stand in a straight line and bow. The cast exit stage right. Music is played.)

Me In The Mirror

"My nose is too big and flat." "My Lips! Please don't hang lips." " I'm too short!" A play about ten children who go through a metamorphosis from self-hate to self-appreciation and love of themselves regardless of their appearance. Excellent play that builds high self-esteem and a better appreciation of Black culture.

Starring

_____GIRL 1

_____GIRL 2

_____GIRL 3

_____GIRL 4

_____GIRL 5

_____GIRL 6

_____GIRL 7

_____BOY 1

_____BOY 2

_____BOY 3

_____BOY 4

Director _____

Stagehands_____

Date _____ Time _____

Place _____

You may photocopy or make a ticket and program like these for your performance of **Me In The Mirror.**

Admit One

Me In The Mirror

Date _____ Time _____

Place _____

Admit One

Seat _____

Admit One

Me In The Mirror

Date _____ Time _____

Place _____

Admit One

Seat _____

Admit One

Me In The Mirror

Date _____ Time _____

Place _____

Admit One

Seat _____

Admit One

Me In The Mirror

Date _____ Time _____

Place _____

Admit One

Seat _____

Admit One

Me In The Mirror

Date _____ Time _____

Place _____

Admit One

Seat _____

Admit One

Me In The Mirror

Date _____ Time _____

Place _____

Admit One

Seat _____

Admit One

Me In The Mirror

Date _____ Time _____

Place _____

Admit One

Seat _____

Admit One

Me In The Mirror

Date _____ Time _____

Place _____

Admit One

Seat _____

Admit One

Me In The Mirror

Date _____ Time _____

Place _____

Admit One

Seat _____

Admit One

Me In The Mirror

Date _____ Time _____

Place _____

Admit One

Seat _____

Admit One

Me In The Mirror

Date _____ Time _____

Place _____

Admit One

Seat _____

Admit One

Me In The Mirror

Date _____ Time _____

Place _____

Admit One

Seat _____

You may photocopy or make a ticket and program like these for your performance of **Me In The Mirror.**

GrandMa

"With Age Comes Wisdom"

A young girl, who hates the thought of spending an afternoon with her 'old and gray" grandmother is won over through the grandmother's wonderful true stories of love, joy, and hardships. This warm delightful play teaches a great lesson of respect and care for our precious elders.

Recommended age group: 9-12

Character Outline:

GRANDMA (80 year old) - girl
MAMA - girl
GIRL - girl

Time: Present

Props:
A table for the kitchen.
A rocking chair for Grandma
A small table with a brush on it, placed behind Grandma's rocking chair.
A purse for mother.
Bags of groceries.

(At Rise: Mama and daughter are sitting at the kitchen table. Stage right Grandma is sitting in a rocking chair. She is looking out into the audience. Mama is writing something on a piece of paper. She stands and picks up her purse)

GIRL: (Stands) Mama, please don't!

MAMA: I've got to go out shopping and you're the only one at home.

GIRL: (Walks over to Mama begging) Mama please don't make me stay with her.

MAMA: I'll be right back.

GIRL: (Sits back down at the table) She's so old mama, I don't know what to talk to her about. You know she won't leave me alone. She always wants you to talk to her. Or she will want me to do something, like comb her hair or wash her cloths, or just sit. Mama, please don't do this to me.

MAMA: (Looking at Girl) That is my mother and your grandmother, you better get to know her, she won't be around too much longer. She's lived a long time. Your life time over and over again. You should respect her and try to get to know her.

GIRL: All right, I'll get to know her later, when we're all here together. Please don't leave me alone with her. You know when you go out, your gonna be gone all day.

MAMA: I am not talking about it any more. You will stay at this house with your grandmother today and that is that. Good-bye.

GIRL: Mama . . .!

MAMA: Good-bye. (Mama exits)

GRANDMA: (Calling out to the Girl) Come in here child!

GIRL: (Looks out into the audience) See I knew it, as soon as we were alone she would call me there. (Calling to Grandma) What do you want Ma Dear?

GRANDMA: (Calling back to the girl) I said, I wanted you to come here.

GIRL: (Walk to stage right) All right Ma Dear, I'm coming. I knew it! I knew it! (Stands in front of Grandma) Yes, Ma Dear.

GRANDMA: (Waves at the Girl to sit) Come and sit down beside me child.

GIRL: Yes Ma Dear. (Sits down on the floor next to Grandma)

GRANDMA: (Looking down at the Girl) You think just cause I'm old, I didn't hear you in there. You think my feelings done grown as hard as the corns on my feet.

GIRL: Do you want me to rub your feet Ma Dear?

GRANDMA: No child, I don't want you to rub my feet. You think that I don't know that none of you children around here care about me.

GIRL: (Gets on her knees next to Grandma) Ma Dear! That's not true. We're just busy. We love you.

GRANDMA: (Looking at the Girl in the eyes) Well if you loved me, you would sit with me some time and talk to me. You think I don't like to talk? You think I like sitting in this chair all day, cause my legs too weak to carry me. I remember when I could run for miles. You think I like talking to myself?

GIRL: No Ma Dear.

GRANDMA: (Looks out into the audience) Get the brush child and brush my hair. Brush some of these years away and I'll tell you of days gone and pass.

GIRL: (Stands and picks up a brush that is on a table next to the Grandma) Yes Ma Dear. (She begins brushing Grandma's hair)

GRANDMA: See when I was a girl your age I didn't sit and with my Grandma. She had been long time dead and I was out working in the fields.

GIRL: You didn't go to school?

GRANDMA: Some time and some time I had to work. There was always work to do. Just couldn't sit and watch the television. (Pause. Grandma looks at the Girl and smiles. Then She looks back to the audience)

GIRL: Tell me more Ma Dear.

GRANDMA: I would sneak a tomato in my mouth whenever my Mama wasn't looking. Real fast like. I was the quickest mouth stuffing, chewing little girl anyone saw. (They laugh)

GIRL: Did you dream Ma Dear? (Grandma nodes her head, yes.) I dreamed a lot. I dreamed about all the things that I was going to do when I grew up and move far away.

GIRL: You know that I am going to be rich Ma Dear.

GRANDMA: Child, I use to dream about meeting me a fine man and moving off to the city and having me plenty of children.

GIRL: Was Grandpa a fine man?

GRANDMA: Never saw a man finer in my life. We never did leave that little country town. Stayed there and built a strong family. Now he's gone and I'm so old that I can't even take care of myself. (Pause) Sometime, I just sit and think.

GIRL: About what?

GRANDMA: I think about everything, life and love. My little life, it's been going on for a long time now. Let me tell you something child about love. Love is a scary thing, it comes and it don't ask you politely if it can enter your soul. No love comes and knocks you down and don't pardon itself. You see I never told you this but you are my favorite grand child.

GIRL: No! I don't believe you.

GRANDMA: It's true, you remind me of my sister Jean. She was a smarty pants, always had something to say.

GIRL: I know that I am not a smarty-pants Ma Dear.

GRANDMA: Jean never could just let things rest, had to fix it with her fancy words. Love. Jean loved love. And I see it in you. Not because of them boys you calling, (Girl looks at Grandma amazed) Yeah, I hear that to. I see it in your eyes, your need to be needed, your willingness to give. Child I see it in you, open up a little. Smile a little.

GIRL: I don't think so Ma Dear.

GRANDMA: You may not listen to me now but you just remember what your Grandma told you.

GIRL: I'll try.

GRANDMA: Then you ain't gonna do it. Trying just ain't good enough for me.

GIRL: I'll remember Ma Dear.

GRANDMA: You know child I am 80 years old and I have seen a little bit of everything. I done seen more men, done known more women, felt more pain. Done known hunger in the middle of the night and laughter with the moon and child at this age I still feel something missing. It's a need to share with my children. Share all the living I been doing.

GIRL: I'm listening Ma Dear.

GRANDMA: My life is all I got to give, my stories. You need to know where you came from and where you can go.

GIRL: Ma Dear, I'll to you.

GRANDMA: If I lived a good life with a ninth grade education. Just think what you can do with a high school diploma and a degree from college. If I made it so can you. My stories and my life can teach you that you can never give up.

GIRL: I understand Ma Dear.

GRANDMA: Let me tell you. I can remember back to when my Daddy built that old house up on the hill for my Mama. We thought we really had something. Running pump water that came to the inside the house and the outhouse was built new.

GIRL: Out house?

GRANDMA: Yeah, the bathroom.

GIRL: It wasn't in the house?

GRANDMA: No! Before that it was far back in the woods but my Daddy built a new one. It wasn't so far back in the woods. Real quick to get to, if you know what I mean. I remember when I was 12 they hung that Evans boy. (Looking off with a sad look on her face)

GIRL: Why Ma Dear? How old was he?

GRANDMA: He was about 13 years old and they hung him for nothing. He was in that old sto' and Mr. Henderson thought that boy had touched his little girl; it was really that little girl who had touched him. I can still hear those dogs barking, chasing that boy and then they caught him, beat him almost half to death and hung him. I saw his body just swinging in the wind. (Pause) I remember crying just because I knew the truth and didn't nobody want to listen to me 'cause I was just a little colored girl. (Girl stands just looking at Grandma).

GIRL: Then what Ma Dear?

GRANDMA: Then I think I was about 16 when I meet your Grand Pa. I was standing outside and he was walking pass the house. He saw me and passed that way for a month. Just whistling and walking. (Grandma laughs) Until one day my Daddy stopped him and asked him what he wanted. He told him that he wanted to take me out. I was so surprised. My Daddy call me over and asked me if I wanted to go out with him. I was so nervous. But I didn't let your Grand Pa know I was nervous cause I liked him a lot, a whole lot. (Grandma and Girl laughs together) It was hot too. Did I tell you how hot it was? Musta been a hundred and one degrees that day. I said yes, right away. We went out and 3 months later we were married.

GIRL: At 16 you got married?

GRANDMA: Yeah back in them days 16 was a good marrying age. My Daddy got him extra help on the farm and grand children. Then come your daddy and uncles and aunts. So much happened. I just told you the beginning child.

MAMA: (Enters from stage left calling to girl) I'm home!

GIRL: (Looks at Grandma) I'll be back. (Girl walks over to stage left)

MAMA: (Looking at Girl) Was it really all that bad staying here with your Grandma?

GIRL: (Looking at Mama) No Mama, Ma Dear's been telling me about her life, things I never knew about.

MAMA: Well you can go on and do whatever you want to do. I'll take care of Ma Dear.

GIRL: I think I'll go and brush Ma Dears hair a little more. (Mama looks at Girl with surprise)

GRANDMA: Child, child!

GIRL: I'm coming Ma Dear. I'm coming. (Girl walks over to Grandma and sits next to her. They freeze. Lights go down and they exit.)

(Enters Mama, Girl and Grandma from stage left they hold hand and bow. Exit) The End.

GrandMa

A play about a young girl who hates the thought of spending an afternoon with her 'old and gray" grandmother. She is won over through the grandmother's wonderful true stories of love, joy, and hardships. This warm delightful play teaches a great lesson of respect and care for our precious elders.

Starring

_____GrandMa

_____Mama

_____Girl

Director _____

*Stagehands*_____

Date _____ *Time* _____

Place _____

You may photocopy or make a ticket and program like these for your performance of GrandMa

Admit One		Admit One	
GrandMa	Admit One ___	**GrandMa**	Admit One ___
Date _____ Time _____	Seat ___	Date _____ Time _____	Seat ___
Place _____		Place _____	

Admit One		Admit One	
GrandMa	Admit One ___	**GrandMa**	Admit One ___
Date _____ Time _____	Seat ___	Date _____ Time _____	Seat ___
Place _____		Place _____	

Admit One		Admit One	
GrandMa	Admit One ___	**GrandMa**	Admit One ___
Date _____ Time _____	Seat ___	Date _____ Time _____	Seat ___
Place _____		Place _____	

Admit One		Admit One	
GrandMa	Admit One ___	**GrandMa**	Admit One ___
Date _____ Time _____	Seat ___	Date _____ Time _____	Seat ___
Place _____		Place _____	

Admit One		Admit One	
GrandMa	Admit One ___	**GrandMa**	Admit One ___
Date _____ Time _____	Seat ___	Date _____ Time _____	Seat ___
Place _____		Place _____	

Admit One		Admit One	
GrandMa	Admit One ___	**GrandMa**	Admit One ___
Date _____ Time _____	Seat ___	Date _____ Time _____	Seat ___
Place _____		Place _____	

You may photocopy or make a ticket and program like these for your performance of **GrandMa**

The Slick Kidnapper

"It's A Bad Child Who Does Not Take Advice"

Misty ventures too far from home in the Big City. There she meets a "nice sweet" man full of candy and surprises. Unfortunately, Mr. Slick has evil plans for little Misty. This is a great play that teaches a valuable lesson to all children. - "Your can't trust everyone and believe everything that they tell you, " says Slick.

Recommended age: 8 - 12

Character Outline

Misty - Little girl who is kidnapped.
Mr. Slick - The kidnaper
Witness - The witness to the kidnapping
Mother - Misty's mother
Father - Misty's father
Brother - Misty's brother
Ms. Candice - Old nosy next door neighbor
Ms. Monica - Old nosy and cranky next-door neighbor
Detective - The detective who captures Mr. Slick
Narrator - Person who carries signs

Time: Present

Props:
10 chairs for the cast to sit in while not on the stage.
A chair for the witness
Rope
Toy gun
Phone
Bag of money
Bus stop sign.
The narrator will use signs created by the cast.

Authors Note: The children should make the signs that the narrator will display. Signs should read; The Big City, The Park, The Home Of the Very Bad Man, Mr. Slick and The Home Of the Little Girl, Misty. When I produced this play with a group of children I asked that they really over act.

10 chairs where placed behind the stage. The chairs served two purposes. One, they where used as props during the play. Two, they gave the actors somewhere to sit when not on the stage. As the actor exit the stage they would go and sit in chair until their part.

The stage setting never changes; props are carried onto the stage while the narrator carries the signs. If there is no stage, chairs and props should sit on the side of the play area. Props should be carried in while narrator is a caring sign.

(At rise: A bus stop sign stands center stage. Narrator enters carrying a sign, it reads, ""The Big City." Narrator walks around the complete stage making sure everyone in the audience has read the sign. Enters Witness, the witness sits down and looks from stage left to stage right. Misty enters.)

WITNESS: (Looking at Misty) Little girl, (Misty turns her head, looking away from the witness) where are you going?

MISTY: My mother told me never talk to strangers.

WITNESS: I just want to help you. Where are you going all alone?

MISTY: (Looking at the witness) I'm going to "The Big City."

WITNESS: Where is your mother?

(Misty looks away from the witness.)

WITNESS: Did you hear me little girl?

MISTY: I can go wherever I want; I'm _____ (insert actors age) years old. And I'm old enough to do what I want.

WITNESS: Well, you just wait right here little girl. I'm going to get the police and they'll take you home. Don't you know you can get hurt in "he Big City?"

MISTY: I can take care of myself.

WITNESS: Well you just wait right here. (Witness exits)

MISTY: That old lady is in my business. (Enters the Slick Kidnaper. He passes Misty, stops, thinks, looks out to the audience. Walks backward to Misty.)

MR. SLICK: How are you doing today little girl?

(Misty turns away)

MR. SLICK: Where are you going?

MISTY: My mother told me never talk to strangers.

MR. SLICK: (Smiling) I'm no stranger; I'm your friend. Now where are you going?

MISTY: I'm going to "The Big City" all by myself.

MR. SLICK: Well let me give you a ride.

(Misty shakes her head "no")

I have a car. A real nice car. And I have candy, all the candy you want. Come on. We will have a good time. I can tell that you are a really big girl, going off by yourself. And you're so pretty.

(Misty turns toward Mr. Slick with a smile on her face.)

MISTY: You really think that I'm pretty?

MR. SLICK: Oh yes, you are very pretty. Lets go.

MISTY: (slowly) Well I guess . . . Where's your car and the candy.

MR. SLICK: My car is around the corner and the candy is at my house.

MISTY: I have to be home before dark.

(They begin to slowly walk off the stage.)

MR. SLICK: Of course. By the way what's your name?

MISTY: Misty, and yours?

MR.SLICK: Mr. Slick. But you can just call me Slick. (They exit. Enters Witness.)

WITNESS: Little girl, the police are coming.

(See looks off stage and notices with surprise that Misty is walking with Mr. Slick.)

WITNESS: (Yelling) Stop! You better come back! (Runs off stage)

(Narrator stands and enters the stage. The narrator holds up the sign and walks with sign that reads, "The Home of the Little Girl, Misty." Exits to seat. Enters Mother. She is pacing back and forth looking at her watch.)

MOTHER: Now where is that girl?

(Enters Father)

FATHER: What's wrong?

MOTHER: It's Misty; I've looked everywhere for her. I can't find her. Have you seen her?

FATHER: No!

MOTHER: When she gets home I'm going to . . .

FATHER: Don't worry if she's not home soon I'll call the police.

MOTHER: I'm going outside and wait for her. (Father exits. Mother walks to stage left. She stands looking for Misty. Stage right enters Ms. Candice and Ms. Monica they are two old nosy neighbors.)

MOTHER: Ms. Candice, Ms. Monica, have you seen Misty? She's been gone all day.

MS. CANDICE: No I haven't.

MS. MONIC: Well, you know how children are today. They think they are grown. And that child thinks that she is old as you.

MOTHER: Just tell me if you've seen her!

MS. MONIC: No I haven't.

(Enters Brother bouncing a ball)

MOTHER: Son have you seen Misty?

BROTHER: Yeah, I saw her.

(Pause. They all look at him waiting for him to say something)

MOTHER: Where is she son?

BROTHER: I don't know where she is now, but earlier today, I saw her walking toward "The Big City".

MOTHER: Why didn't you try and stop her?

BROTHER: You know Misty never listens to me.

MOTHER: I've got to call the police. Come on son.

(They all exit.)

(Stage hands quickly place a chair, and table with a phone on it center stage. Narrator enters with sign, " The Home of the Bad Man Mr. Slick" walks around the stage holding up the sign and exits to chair.)

MR. SLICK: Come in Misty.

MISTY: (Looks around) Slick, don't you ever clean your house?

MR. SLICK: No, I don't like cleaning. (Walks over to a small table and gives Misty the candy)

MISTY: Thanks Slick. (Pause) It's getting late I think you should take me home now. (Smiles)

MR. SLICK: Home, you just got here. Why don't you sit down?

(Slick pushes Misty in chair)

MISTY: You don't have to push me Slick.

MR. SLICK: Sit down and relax, let's talk for a while. Get to know one another better. (Slick exits)

MISTY: Ok Slick. Well I live just outside of "The Big City". I really like going to school and I knew. . (Looking around the room) Slick! Slick where are you?

Enters Slick with rope and a gun)

MISTY: Slick what are you going to do?

MR. SLICK: Keep you here with me for a while. (Misty begins to scream. Slick points gun at her)

MR. SLICK: Be quiet! Now I am going to tie you up and then I'm going to make a phone call to your parents. (Mr. Slick ties Misty to chair.) Tell me your phone number.

MISTY: Please Slick don't do this!

MR. SLICK: Just tell me your number!

MISTY: Slick you told me that you where my friend.

MR. SLICK: You can't believe everything everyone tells you, now can you. That's your lesson for today. (Pointing the gun at Misty) What's your number?

MISTY: (Very fast) 552 - 9976!

MR. SLICK: Good. (Places gag in Mist's mouth. Walks over to the phone and picks up the receiver. He begins to dial the number) Listen, I have your sweet little girl. I want one thousand dollars at the park tomorrow or your sweet little girl will pay. Put the money in a paper bag and leave it by the swings. And you better not call the police. (Hangs up the phone and laughs really bud. Misty sits scared and crying. Slick walks back to Misty and turns chair around so that her back is to the audience. As he exits he pushes Misty's chair to the side of the stage. They both exit stage)

(Enters narrator with the next sign it reads, " The Home of the Little Girl, Misty" walks around the stage and exits.)

(Enters Mother she is crying. Father enters bringing in a chair for Mother.)

MOTHER: What are we going to do? (Sits down)

FATHER: The police are sending a detective over to the house.

MOTHER: You heard what he said.

FATHER: We have to do something; I think that a detective will be able to get our little girl back. This guy is just small town he only wants one thousand dollars.

MOTHER: Small town or big he could hurt our little girl.

(Doorbell rings)

MOTHER: I'll get it.

(Mother walks to stage right act as though she is opening a door. Enters the detective)

DETECTIVE JONES: Hello, I'm detective Jones, you called about a missing little girl.

MOTHER: (Crying) Yes, this very bad man has our little girl.

FATHER: He called and wanted one thousand dollars at the park tomorrow.

DETECTIVE JONES: What else did he say?

MOTHER: He said that he would hurt our little girl.

DETECTIVE JONES: Don't worry. I'll handle everything. Now, listen his is what we are going to do.

(They all huddle up close together and begin to whisper. They exit to seats.)

(Enters Narrator with the next sign it reads, "The Park.")

(Enters Mother with a paper bag. She walks to center stage, looks around and puts the bag down and walks back to stage left. Enters Mr. Slick with Misty from stage left, they walk pass Mother. Misty looks at her mother and begins to cry. Slick whispers in Mist's ear, she stands near center stage. He walks over to the bag bends down, grabs the bag. He stands, and begins to walks away. Enter Detective Jones from stage right.)

DETECTIVE JONES: Stop! Stop! (Mr. Slick runs off stage.

Detective Jones runs after him off stage.)

MISTY: Mama! Mama! (Enter Father and Brother)

MOTHER AND FATHER: Misty!

(Misty, Mother, Father and Brother hug.)

FATHER: Misty are you all right?

MISTY: Yes.

MOTHER: I hope you learned a lesson from this little girl.

MISTY: Yes, I learned never to talk to strangers and never to go off into "The Big City" all by myself.

FATHER: Let's go home.

(They all slowly exit but before they are off stage enters the Detective with Mr. Slick)

DETECTIVE JONES: And we hope that you've learned a lesson to.

(Cast walks to center stage, holds hands and bows)

The End.

The Slick Kidnapper

Misty ventures too far from home in the Big City. There she meets a "nice sweet" man full of candy and surprises. Unfortunately, Mr. Slick has evil plans for little Misty. This is a great play that teaches a valuable lesson to all children. - "Your can't trust everyone and believe everything that they tell you, " says Slick.

Starring

_____Misty

_____Mr. Slick

_____Witness

_____Father

_____Brother

_____Ms. Candice

_____Ms. Monica

_____Detective

_____Narrator

Director _____

*Stagehands*_____

Date _____ *Time* _____

Place _____

*You may photocopy or make a ticket and program like these for your performance of **The Slick Kidnapper**.*

Admit One	
The Slick Kidnapper	Admit One ___
Date _____ Time _____	Seat ___
Place _____	

Admit One	
The Slick Kidnapper	Admit One ___
Date _____ Time _____	Seat ___
Place _____	

Admit One	
The Slick Kidnapper	Admit One ___
Date _____ Time _____	Seat ___
Place _____	

Admit One	
The Slick Kidnapper	Admit One ___
Date _____ Time _____	Seat ___
Place _____	

Admit One	
The Slick Kidnapper	Admit One ___
Date _____ Time _____	Seat ___
Place _____	

Admit One	
The Slick Kidnapper	Admit One ___
Date _____ Time _____	Seat ___
Place _____	

Admit One	
The Slick Kidnapper	Admit One ___
Date _____ Time _____	Seat ___
Place _____	

Admit One	
The Slick Kidnapper	Admit One ___
Date _____ Time _____	Seat ___
Place _____	

Admit One	
The Slick Kidnapper	Admit One ___
Date _____ Time _____	Seat ___
Place _____	

Admit One	
The Slick Kidnapper	Admit One ___
Date _____ Time _____	Seat ___
Place _____	

Admit One	
The Slick Kidnapper	Admit One ___
Date _____ Time _____	Seat ___
Place _____	

Admit One	
The Slick Kidnapper	Admit One ___
Date _____ Time _____	Seat ___
Place _____	

*You may photocopy or make a ticket and program like these for your performance of **The Slick Kidnapper.***

Back To The Past

"A People Without A Knowledge Of Their History,
Is Like A Tree Without Roots."

An exciting play that takes 13 children on a unforgettable adventure "Back To The Past" to meet famous, not so famous and great African American achievers. Bessie Smith, Marcus Garvey, and Matthew Henson are just a few who visit and teach the children about their beautiful past.

Recommended Age Group: 9-14

Character Outline

MS. WEBSTER - very mean, strict teacher
STUDENT - Introduces the play
STUDENT 1 - Boy
STUDENT 2 - Girl
STUDENT 3 - Boy
STUDENT 4 - Boy
STUDENT 5 - Girl

Historical Characters
MARY BETHUNE
FREDERICK DOUGLAS
MATTHEW HENSON
BESSIE MAE SMITH
MARCUS GARVEY
HARRIET TUBMAN
DENMARK VESY

Time: Present.

Props:
5 desks for students
History books, pen and small note pad.
Historical characters may dress in costumes or they may wear black.

(At Rise: Historical characters enter, they sit in the front row with the audience. Student enters stands center stage.)

STUDENT: (To the audience) You have now entered the classroom of Ms. Webster. (Enters Ms. Webster from stage right walking very fast. She stands at center stage left. She's looks at the audience with a very mean expression on her face.) She, (Pause, looks at Ms. Webster) is a very mean woman. She has very little respect for children. I think she just doesn't understand us. These are her students. (Enter students with history books. They sit in desk or chairs and look out into the audience.) This class is history. These students, are looking for the truth. A history that includes everyone. To find it, they must go on a daring adventure, " back to the past." Meeting famous and not so famous historical characters, who leads them to the truth.

(Student exits stage right. Ms. Webster walks to the front of the classroom. The side of Ms. Webster is seen by the audience)

MS. WEBSTER: Tonight for your homework you will read pages 110 - 210.

STUDENT 1: That's 100 pages!

MS. WEBSTER: Good, you can count.

(STUDENT 3 raises hand)

MS. WEBSTER: Yes. (Pointing to STUDENT 3)

STUDENT 3: I didn't understand what we read last night.

MS. WEBSTER: Then read it again.

STUDENT 2: It didn't make any sense to me either.

STUDENT 5: Can you please tell us about some black people in history?

MS. WEBSTER: No, that is not a part of our reading. We will cover that when the time comes.

STUDENT 4: We want to know what some black people did. We are reading world history and black people have always been in the world. That's what my Uncle Abdule said.

STUDENT 1: My mama told me that too.

STUDENT 4: So why aren't there more black people in our history book.

MS. WEBSTER: Who would like to leave the room for causing trouble? You must raise your hand before I will answer any of your questions.

(All the students raise there hands)

MS. WEB STER: No time for questions.

STUDENT 1: You said . . .

MS. WEBSTER: Listen people, we have to learn about history.

STUDENT 3: Did Black people create anything? Did we climb any mountains?

STUDENT 1: This just don't seem right to me. I know we did something besides just being slaves.

MS. WEBSTER: That will be enough. The bell, will ring in 3 minutes. I want you to put away your books and begin writing a paper for me titled "Why I should raise my hand before talking in class." (Students moan and groan about the work assigned. Each student begins to take out a piece of paper. The bell rings.)

MS. WEBSTER: Class dismissed. (She exits stage right.)

(Students stand, looking at history books)

STUDENT 1: This can't be history.

STUDENT 2: I want a book that talks about me, for me.

STUDENT 3: Well, I guess we better go.

STUDENT 4: There just ain't no truth in this book. I ain't reading it.

STUDENT 5: We should. . . throw these book down. And never pick them up again.

STUDENT 2: What?

STUDENT 4: Yeah that's right.

STUDENT 1: I can't believe you said that. You never say a word, your so shy.

(STUDENT 5 nods his head yes)

STUDENT 5: We'll pick them up when somebody decides to tell us the truth.

STUDENT 3: How will we know the truth?

STUDENT 1: Easter bunny.

STUDENT 5: Santa Clause.

STUDENT 4: Tooth Fairy.

STUDENT 3: How will we know the truth?

STUDENT 3: Let's do it.

STUDENT 2: What if we get in trouble? Like, kicked out of school.

STUDENT 4: So What!

STUDENT 2: So what? So my Mama is going to get me.

STUDENT 5: I heard somebody say, if you don't stand for something you'll fall for anything.

STUDENT 3: What does that mean?

STUDENT 4: It means throw the book down.

STUDENT 3: Now?

STUDENT 4: Let's do it, now.

(STUDENTS hold their books high above their heads and one by one they drop their books. After the last book drops lights begin to dim. Authors Note: If your lights do not dim, continue on with the play, acting as if lights have dimmed)

STUDENT 4: (Looking down at the books) There just ain't no truth in it.

(They all shake their heads in anger and sadness.)

STUDENT 1: (Looking around) Look! It's getting dark in here.

STUDENT 4: (Yells out) Who's playing with the lights?

(They all stand around looking at one another scared)

STUDENT 2: We're the only ones in here.

STUDENT 5: I'm getting scared. Let's get out of here!

(They all look around.)

STUDENT 1: (Starts to run around) Let's go!

STUDENT 2: (excited) Do we leave the books here?

STUDENT 5: Forget those books, let's go!

(STUDENTS act as of they are going to run)

STUDENT 3:Go where? I can't see anything. I can see you (pointing at other students) but I can't see anything else around us.

STUDENT 5: This is scary.

STUDENT 4: This is weird, very weird.

MARY BETHUNE:: (From the front row) Pick up those books!

STUDENT 1: Did you hear that?

(Children stand looking around. Mary Bethune step forward to the children. Children jump back startled by Mary Bethune.)

MARY BETHUNE:: I told you children to pick up those books. (Points to books)

STUDENT 3: Who are you?

MARY BETHUNE:: I am a part of your history, a part of the truth.

STUDENT 2: She's somebody we should know.

STUDENT 1: I never saw her on television.

MARY BETHUNE:: I never been on television.

STUDENT 5: Who are you?

MARY BETHUNE:: I am Mary Bethune.

STUDENT 5: Where did you come from?

MARY BETHUNE:: From your wants, from your needs. You needed to know, so I came to you. Now pick up those books.

STUDENT 5: That book doesn't include us.

STUDENT 1: It talks about the same people, Martin Luther King, Michael Jackson, and a few slaves.

MARY BETHUNE:: Those are important people. They are apart of your history.

STUDENT 4: Yeah, but there's more history than that.

STUDENT 2: We want to know the whole story, our story.

STUDENT 3: Like you. The book doesn't say much about you.

(STUDENT 4 bends down, picks up book and opens it to a page and reads.)

STUDENT 4: This book says that you where born in 1875 and died in 1955. It also says that you began your own university.

(MARY BETHUNE: nods her head "yes" as he is reading)

STUDENT 2: The book says you died. How can you be here with us if you are died?

STUDENT 3: I'm getting scared again.

MARY BETHUNE: Not even death can hold the truth. I have come to you to tell you the truth. Now, what else does that book say about me?

STUDENT 4: That's all.

MARY BETHUNE:: That's all? There's more to me than when I lived and when I died. Does it tell you how I got the money for that school?

(Student's looks down in the book then they look up and say together "NO")

STUDENT 1: Tell us.

MARY BETHUNE:: I sold sweet potato pies.

STUDENT 4: I bet that was some good pie.

MARY BETHUNE: Good enough to build a university. When I left home in 1904 to start my school do you know how much money I had in my pocket purse? I had $1.50 that's all. I was determined. I founded the National Counsel of Negro Women and my school Bethune-Cookman College. I worked and believed in the education of my people, in my children. There where many more who believed. Fannie Coppin believed.

STUDENT 5: Who was she?

MARY BETHUNE:: Pick up those books and look. Just keep asking. You'll get the truth one way or another. (STUDENT 2 bends down and picks up his book and looks at every page.)

STUDENT 2: She's not in our book.

MARY BETHUNE:: She, is one of the forgotten ones. Those left out of the history books. You can't see them. But they are all around you. (Children look around) The important people history forgot. (Mary Bethune begins to walks toward the audience speaking as she is walking) Standing waiting, wanting to be known, wanting to know that their living was not in vain. (Exit's stage, stands in front of her chair) You'll meet them, just keep on looking. (Sits down)

STUDENT 3: (Calling in the direction of the audience) Ms. Bethune can you tell us where to look?

STUDENT 1: (Calling out) Can you please tell us where we are? It's so dark.

STUDENT 2: Ms. Bethune!

STUDENT 4: She's gone.

STUDENT 5: (Crying) Now what do we do?

STUDENT 4: You can't start crying. How will that help?

STUDENT 5: I can cry if I want to.

(Enters Harriet Tubman running from her seat calling to the children)

HARRIET TUBMAN: Get down children, get down! Be careful and don't you cry. (Children squat down. The historical characters repeat after Harriet Tubman, "Get down Children, get down" twice. The historical characters sit with backs to chairs) The cries of my people been calling me for centuries. Tell them the hardest times are behind them. I carried people to freedom and I never lost one. I led more than 300 of my people to freedom. Through that underground railroad.

STUDENT 3: A railroad under the ground?

HARRIET TUBMAN: (Laughs) No child, the underground railroad was black people and white people. They knew that slavery was wrong. They helped slaves to freedom. With their help, dogs, guns and mad men couldn't stop me.

STUDENT 2: I think somebody should write all this down.

STUDENT 3: (Pulls out pen and a small pad from his pocket) I'll write!

STUDENT 1: I know you. (He stands) You are Harriet Tubman.

HARRIET TUBMAN: Get down. (STUDENT 1 squats back down) You write this down and tell the truth. I was doing what I had to for you, for your future. (Student 3 is writing as fast as he can) I got to go now but you tell them the truth.

(Staying very low Harriet Tubman begins to walks to chair)

STUDENT 5: Tell who?

HARRIET TUBMAN: (Turns and looks at the children) Everyone that you know, everyone that you meet.

STUDENT 3: Slow down I can't write that fast.

HARRIET TUBMAN: I got to go. Got a meeting to attend to. Take care children. (Walks of stage very fast and returns to seat in front row)

(Student 3 stops writing)

STUDENT 5: (Stands, calls out to the front row with hands cupped around his mouth) Ms. Tubman can you tell us where we are?

HARRIET TUBMAN: (From the front row) You here and there, past and present. You where you supposed to be.

(Students slowly stand together)

STUDENT 3: (To Student 1) Did you see where she went?

STUDENT 1: No, I didn't. No one is going to believe this.

STUDENT 4: Meeting dead people from the past, it's going to be a hard story to tell.

STUDENT 5: (looking out toward the audience) I want to go home.

STUDENT 4: Well go. See if you can find your way out of this darkness.

STUDENT 5: All right, who wants to help me find the light switch?

STUDENT 2: I ain't going no where with you.

STUDENT 3: Ms. Tubman said we where we're supposed to be.

STUDENT 4: You go by yourself.

STUDENT 5: (Whining) I can't go by myself. I just want to get out of here. Can we just walk together? I just want to go home.

STUDENT 2: All right.

(The Students begin to walk, they take 3 very careful steps. They are moving very slow and standing close together. With eyes opened wide they are looking in all directions)

(The voice of Marcus Garvey is heard from the front row)

MARCUS GARVEY:: Back home, where is home?

(Student's stop walking)

STUDENT 3: Home is _____ (Name of the city where the actors live)

STUDENT 5: Who said that?

STUDENT 1: Be quiet.

MARCUS GARVEY: (Enters Marcus Garvey) Students jump back startled and amazed.) I was going to take my people home on a fleet of steam ships, "The Black Star Line." The home land, Africa. My name is Marcus Garvey.

STUDENT 2: You writing this down.

STUDENT 3: (Begins to write) Wait it's happening too fast. (Spelling out the letters) M-arcus G-a-rvey.

STUDENT 4: Now, I know you weren't in our history book.

MARCUS GARVEY: I was born in Jamaica in 1887 I died in 1940. I came to the United States to help my people and to one day carry them home. With the help of others, I established the Universal Negro Improvement Association. We set up grocery stores, restaurants and a newspaper.

STUDENT 4: What happened?

STUDENT 3: He died.

MARCUS GARVEY:: Yes, I did die. But before that I help thousands of people. There where many who where on my side. They gave money to many of my organizations. The government of this the United States felt that I was keeping this money for myself. They said that I did not pay my taxes. That I was cheating the people. So I was deported.

STUDENT 3: (Looking at students) Somebody, spell deported.

MARCUS GARVEY: Forced from my work and my mission, back to my home of Jamaica. My dream was never fulfilled and now I sit. There have been many books written about me. I want you, the children, to know that you must build your own schools, stores, and lives. (Walks to chair, stands in front of the chair) Remember, build your own. (Sits down)

(The historical characters echo Marcus Garvey, " Build Your Own". The children act as though they are startled by the voices.)

STUDENT 1: Where did he go?

STUDENT 2: I don't know!

STUDENT 3: What was the last thing that he said?

STUDENT 5: He said build your own.

STUDENT 4: Now we know, to look for the truth and build our own.

STUDENT 2: Should we build our own truth?

STUDENT 4: No!

STUDENT 2: Then what should we do?

STUDENT 5: I don't know but I know that I'm getting hungry.

STUDENT 3: I'm tired of writing.

STUDENT 2: I want to see some light. I'm tired of this darkness and dead people, I'm getting depressed.

STUDENT 4: We got to learn this. We got to know this so we can tell the truth.

STUDENT 1: This could go on forever.

STUDENT 3: Let's go I'm tired.

STUDENT 5: I'm hungry.

STUDENT 2: And I'm depressed.

(BESSIE MAE SMITH: begins to hum while sitting in the front row)

STUDENT 4: (With anticipation) All right, get ready to write.

STUDENT 3: (To Student 4) You write!

STUDENT 4: (To Student 3) You said you wanted to write.

(Enters Bessie Mae Smith with her hands on her hips and a very large hat on her head. She is singing and humming. She walks toward the children. The children step back, looking at Bessie Mae Smith up and down)

BESSIE MAE SMITH: (Very sassy) Now stop fighting. You all have got what I call "the blues." Don't fight sing. Children looking at me so strange, you don't know who I am? (Students shake their heads no) I sang the blues. I'm still singing it, they call me Bessie Mae Smith. My voice was so strong, I didn't even need a microphone. My songs where about the sadness of my people. I sang about poverty, racism and love. I was one of the greatest blues singers.You didn't know that did you?

STUDENT 5: No.

BESSIE MAE SMITH: Now you do. Write about me in all the history books. Did you write it?

STUDENT 3: I wrote it.

BESSIE MAE SMITH: That's good enough for me. Now put me in

the books, cause the blues was important to our people. It was our own creation. Don't let nobody tell you anything else. Remember honeys, remember the past and don't forget us. (She places her hands on her hips and begins to hum.)

STUDENT 2: What song are you humming Ms. Smith?

BESSIE MAE SMITH: Just an old song that I remember. (Walks to her chair with her hands on her hips humming. Talks while she is walking) Children take care of yourselves and remember what I said. (Sits down)

STUDENT 4: I liked her.

STUDENT 2: I just bet you did.

STUDENT 5: I wonder if we know enough to go home now.

STUDENT 1: This could go on forever.

STUDENT 4: (Looking in the direction of the historical characters) Truth, build your own, and remember.

(The historical characters echoes Student 4 from the front row, "Remember" 3 times)

STUDENT 2: Where are those voices coming from? They are driving me crazy.

STUDENT 1: (yelling into the darkness) Who are you? (All children begin to ask "Who are you?" 5 times. The children's voices become a whisper and then silence.)

BENJAMIN BANNEKER: (Stands and walks to the children. Stands center stage. Children step back looking amazed) Benjamin Banneker, stargazer. I perfected the clock. I built one that kept perfect time for more than 50 years.

FREDERICK DOUGLAS: (Stand walks toward the children. Stands next to Benjamin Banneker) Frederick Douglas, a voice of freedom. Through my moving words people who had never experienced slavery, understood it with sadness and disgrace. I established the North Star newspaper and was appointed minister to Haiti. Still today my words move readers.

MATTHEW HENSON: (Stands walks toward the children. Stands on the opposite side of Benjamin Banneker)

MATTHEW HENSON: a great explorer. On April the 6th I placed the American flag on the North pole. It took the world 81 years to recognize the great things I did.

DENMARK VESEY: (Stands and walks forward to the children. Stands next to Matthew Henson)Denmark Vesy, Lover of Freedom. A dedicated fighter against slavery. I planned an uprising that would free slaves in the city of Charleston. Although my plan was discovered and I was hung, my efforts helped focus attention on the struggle against slavery.

BENJAMIN BANNEKER: (Walks back to chair in the front row) Inventors.

(Sits down)

FREDERICK DOUGLAS::: (Walks back to chair in the front row) Writers.

(Sits down)

DENMARK VESY: (Walks back to chair in the front row) Freedom fighters.

(Sits down)

MATTHEW HENSON: (Walks back to chair in the front row) Builders of tomorrow. (Sits down)

(Students and historical characters chants like the beat of a drum. "Truth, truth" 3 times. (Silent pause) The children stand amazed.)

STUDENT 3: Now, we know some of the truth.

STUDENT 4: Truth.

STUDENT 5: Yeah, now we have a beginning. We know that we must remember those who have gone before us and always look for the truth.

(They pick up their books and all of a sudden they can see everything around them. They see the door and stand in amazement.)

STUDENT 1: Look everybody, I can see the door.

STUDENT 2: It's the classroom. . .

STUDENT 5: (With joy) All right, we're back!

(Enter Ms. Webster walking at a very fast pace. She stops shocked to see the children.)

MS. WEBSTER: Students, don't you have a home?

STUDENT 4: That was a REAL history lesson.

STUDENT 2: Now, we know the truth.

(Students stand looking at Ms. Webster smiling.)

MS. WEBSTER: Go home, just go home. Truth indeed. Truth.

(Children smile and exit stage right)

MARY BETHUNE:: (Stands) The Truth . . .

MS. WEBSTER: Who was that? (Looking out in the audience)

(Ms. Webster quickly exits. Mary Bethune sits. Historical characters stand and walk to the stage together, hold hands and bow. They exit the stage or play area. Enter Students, they stand center stage, hold hands and bow. They exit) THE END

Back To The Past

An exciting play that takes 13 children on a unforgettable adventure "Back To The Past" to meet famous, not so famous and great African American achievers. Bessie Smith, Marcus Garvey, and Matthew Henson are just a few who visit and teach the children about their beautiful past

Starring

Historical Characters

_____Ms. Webster ——————————Mary Bethune

_____Student ——————————Federick Douglas

_____Student 1 ——————————Matthew Henson

_____Student 2 ——————————Bessie Mae Smith

_____Student 3 ——————————Marcus Garvey

_____Student 4 ——————————Harriet Tubman

_____Student 5 ——————————Denmark Vesy

Director _____

Stagehands_____

Date _____ Time _____

Place _____

*You may photocopy or make a ticket and program like these for your performance of **Back To The Past.***

Admit One		Admit One	
Back To The Past	Admit One ___ Seat ___	**Back To The Past**	Admit One ___ Seat ___
Date _____ Time _____		Date _____ Time _____	
Place _____		Place _____	

Admit One		Admit One	
Back To The Past	Admit One ___ Seat ___	**Back To The Past**	Admit One ___ Seat ___
Date _____ Time _____		Date _____ Time _____	
Place _____		Place _____	

Admit One		Admit One	
Back To The Past	Admit One ___ Seat ___	**Back To The Past**	Admit One ___ Seat ___
Date _____ Time _____		Date _____ Time _____	
Place _____		Place _____	

Admit One		Admit One	
Back To The Past	Admit One ___ Seat ___	**Back To The Past**	Admit One ___ Seat ___
Date _____ Time _____		Date _____ Time _____	
Place _____		Place _____	

Admit One		Admit One	
Back To The Past	Admit One ___ Seat ___	**Back To The Past**	Admit One ___ Seat ___
Date _____ Time _____		Date _____ Time _____	
Place _____		Place _____	

Admit One		Admit One	
Back To The Past	Admit One ___ Seat ___	**Back To The Past**	Admit One ___ Seat ___
Date _____ Time _____		Date _____ Time _____	
Place _____		Place _____	

*You may photocopy or make a ticket and program like these for your performance of **Back To The Past**.*

Kwanzaa: A Time For Change

"Kwanzaa is the wonderful African celebration of life, harvest, and good fortunes."

This play introduces children and adults to the true meaning of Kwanzaa. The main character, James, refuses to join the family's celebration of Kwanzaa and learns the difficult way that Kwanzaa is truly a beautiful family celebration.

Recommended Age Group: 9-14

CHARACTER OUTLINE

MAMA - Mother
DADDY - Father
JAMES - Oldest Brother
HOWARD - Middle Brother
JESS - The Youngest Brother

Time: Present

Props:
Couch
Table With 5 Chairs
Plates with plastic foods
Kinar (candle holder)
Mkeke (straw mat)
Mishuma Saba (3 red candles, 3 green candles, & 1 black candle)
Small bowl filled with pop corn
3 ears of corn
Business coat for Daddy
Book
Telephone (small table for phone)
Basket
Crate
Paper (red, green, and gold)

ACT 1 SCENE 1

(At rise. The house of the Bell family. The living room and dining room can be seen. Jess and Howard are sitting in the living room. They are all looking very sad. Enter James he is very happy, singing.)

JAMES: Yeah, yeah, James is in the house. Why you looking so glum? (Looks around the room) Where is the tree?

HOWARD: Ain't no tree.

JESS: Yeah ain't no tree.

HOWARD: Man I told you about repeating everything I say.

JAMES: Wait a minute Mutt and Jeff. What you talking about? We always have a tree. It's Christmas, you know x-mas time, joy to the world, Ho HO, Chimneys or for people without a chimney the back door.

HOWARD: We gonna do something different this year.

JAMES: Different?

JESS: Different.

HOWARD: (Stands) See man don't that get on your nerves. Little boy don't have a thought of his own.

JESS: (Stands) Yes I do.

HOWARD: Prove it.

JESS: (Looking around thinking) Well.

HOWARD: See I told you.

JAMES: What we gonna do different?

HOWARD: K - w - a - n - z - a -a. (Sits back down on the couch)

JESS: Kwanzaa. (Sits down on couch)

(Howard acts as if he is going to hit JESS.)

JAMES: Man, leave him alone. What is this Kwanzaa?

JESS: MAMA said it was something for us.

JAMES: Us, us who?

HOWARD: Black people, it's a celebration for us.

JAMES: Wait a minute we not going to get any gifts.

JESS: No gift! Howard we're not going to get any gifts!

(Enters Mama see is singing and wrapping her head with African cloth.)

JAMES: Mama what's this about no Christmas, we got to have Christmas.

MAMA: No we don't have to have nothing and this year we are going to do something different. Start a new tradition for the Bell family.

JESS: See different.

HOWARD: (Stands walks over to Mama) Mama, make Jess stop that.

MAMA: Stop what Howard?

HOWARD: Stop repeating us.

MAMA: Your brother just admires you Howard.

JESS: (stands) No I don't!

MAMA: Yes you do.

JESS: No I don't!

MAMA: Well then stop playing the repeat game with him.

JAMES: Here's my list Mama, everything that I want this year. (Hands her a piece of paper)

MAMA: Want, for what?

JAMES: Christmas, I know you just joking.

(Mama turns and looks at James with a very straight face.)

MAMA: Now does it look like I am joking?

HOWARD: Look at her she got that African thing tied around her head.

MAMA: What is wrong with you. Have I left you so uneducated? I see you sporting your red, gold, green and black.

JAMES: Yeah Mama but that's just a fashion thing. Everybody is wearing it. It don't mean that we can't have Christmas.

HOWARD: What kind of December is this going to be with no Christmas? I beat we ain't gonna have no dinner or family or good times.

MAMA: You are wrong. You see I don't know that much about Kwanzaa myself . . .

JESS: Then why we doing it MAMA. We know about Christmas.

MAMA: But we are all going to learn something wonderful together starting today.

JAMES: MAMA does DADDY know about this wonderful different thing you want to do this year.

MAMA: Why?

JAMES: Because you know how much DADDY just loves Christmas.

JESS: DADDY loves Christmas.

MAMA: Boy!

HOWARD: See Mama I told you.

MAMA: Your Daddy and I have agreed on this change.

JAMES: Man! We gonna be the only family without Christmas.

MAMA: You are going to have something better than Christmas.

JAMES: I'm gonna go over to Chuckies house, I know they doing Christmas. I saw his Ma putting up a nice tree.

MAMA: Listen to me boy, we are going to celebrate Kwanzaa together and if you don't like it you can stay in your room until it is over do you understand me? And that could be a very long time.

(James sits on couch in anger)

MAMA: That goes for everyone. Dinner will be on the table in 15 minutes go and wash up HOWARD, JAMES and yes even you Mr. Repeat.

JESS: Oh Mama, I don't repeat I'm just listening.

(The boys stand and walk off stage mumbling. Mama stands fixing her head wrap. Enters Daddy from work.)

DADDY: Daddy's in the house!

MAMA: Hello.

DADDY: That's all just, hello. Where are the smiles that use to great me?

MAMA: We have been discussing our change this year to Kwanzaa instead of Christmas and it has been meet with a little disagreement.

DADDY: Just give them sometime and they'll get the idea.

(Mama walks over to the dinner table sets out the plates walks off stage and returns with bowls of food)

MAMA: Dinner! (Exits off stage again)

(They all slowly enter. Each boy sits and has his head hanging down.)

DADDY: No hello for your DADDY boys?

JESS: Heah Daddy

HOWARD: Yeah, heah Dad.

JAMES: Same for me.

DADDY: Now this is not the family that I am accustom to seeing when I get home.

HOWARD: Daddy it's this change that got us all bugged out.

JAMES: Daddy you got to do something about this Kwanzaa thing.

JESS: We want Christmas.

DADDY: Let me ask you a few questions boys. Why do you want Christmas so bad?

JAMES: We always had Christmas Dad.

HOWARD: You know gift giving and eating.

JESS: Gift giving.

DADDY: And why do we give these gifts?

JESS: Because you love us.

DADDY: I love you every day of the year.

JAMES: You want to show it in a very special way.

HOWARD: You know Daddy the tree and everything. It just won't be the same.

JAMES: Now we know Dad, we know the true meaning of Christmas, we saw it on that television special last year. Caring, sharing and giving to the poor - we know all about that stuff.

DADDY: Sons we have to start thinking for ourselves wanting to create something that represents our history and culture. Christmas does not do that. Who do you see on all those specials? Your Santa . . .

(Enters MAMA with a plate of food)

MAMA: Your Santa is that black man sitting at the end of this table.

JESS: No, don't say that Mama!

MAMA: Stop that Jess, we told you years ago that there was and never will be a Santa Claus. Just try it boys, open your mind.

DADDY: There's just one day of Christmas but there are Seven days of Kwanzaa.

HOWARD: (Sadly) Yeah seven.

JAMES: What about the gifts?

MAMA: What about the gifts James?

JESS: Do we get any?

MAMA: Yes, you get gifts but you make the gifts that you give.

HOWARD: Make! What about shopping, you remember shopping Ma'. The mall, the beautiful mall at Christmas time. And the people you remember the people, looking and shopping and buying and buying and shopping, the joy of Christmas.

JESS: The joy of Christmas.

MAMA: Well ain't gonna be no joy like that this year.

HOWARD: But Ma' . . .

DADDY: That's it, no more talking. We all have to grow, reach out in life and try new things. This is our time to do something new something . . .

(All three boys say this line at the same time)

Together: Different!

(MAMA and DADDY look at one another. Shake their heads lights go down.)

End of Act I Scene I

Act I Scene II

(The lights come on to Jess and Howard are sitting in the living room. They are looking around looking around the room waiting. James enters)

JAMES: What's wrong with yawl? You can't move? Why you just gonna sit there?

HOWARD: MAMA told us to.

JESS: You got to come and sit to.

(On the table there is a straw mat, the Kinara, the candleholder with seven candles, Mishumaa Saba, in it. Three red, three green and one black.)

JAMES: (Looking at the table) What's this?

HOWARD: The stuff.

JESS: The stuff.

(Howard and James look at Jess.)

JAMES: What's this stuff for?

(Enter MAMA and DADDY)

MAMA: It's the stuff we use to celebrate Kwanzaa. Everything represents something else. (She sits next to the table) The straw mat or Mkeke it stands for our past. The candleholder or the Kinara is the holder of the flame. It stands for black people past and present. The candles or the Mishumaa Saba stand for the seven principles of Kwanzaa - the principles that we should live by.

HOWARD: (Stands) Now is that it, can we go now?

DADDY: Sit down boy.

(Howard sits)

MAMA: (To Jess) Pass me that basket filled with corn.

JESS: We just ate.

(Jess passes basket of corn to MAMA.)

MAMA: (To JESS) Shhhhh. This is a symbol of the African harvest and thanksgiving. I will put ears of corn on the table. Pass me the ears of corn Howard.

(Howard stands and gets the ears of corn and passes them to his Mama.)

DADDY: The corn represents the number of children in the home. We will place 3 ears of corn on the table. To day everyone will think of gifts that they can make. Did you hear me boys? You make the gifts. The night before the last night of Kwanzaa we give our gifts to one another.

JESS: What can I make?

HOWARD: Who cares?

DADDY: Listen I want to see a change in your attitudes right now or you won't see the light of day except through that window.

JESS: You can make whatever you want.

JAMES: Can we go now?

MAMA: No! There are seven days of Kwanzaa the seven days represent the principles that we should live by. The first day is Umoja- lets all say that together.

HOWARD: Ma!

MAMA: Umoja, say it.

(They all repeat Umoja but with very little energy.)

MAMA: Umoja means unity.

JESS: Unity.

MAMA: The second day is Kujichagulia that means self-determination. Lets all say Kujichagulia.

(They repeat after Mama again with very little energy Kujichagulia.)

MAMA: The third day is Ujima, this means collective works and responsibility. Ujima everyone say it.

(They all repeat Ujima. James and Howard are looking around as if they are bored and tired. Jess is listening intently.)

MAMA: Are you paying attention to me boys? James, Howard do you hear me? I am going to ask you what these mean, so you better listen. The third day is Ujamma, cooperative economics.

JESS: That sounds kind of like the one before.

MAMA: Your right Jess but Ujamma it is spelled U j a m m a. And the Ujima is spelled U j i m a. The fifth day is Nia, purpose.

HOWARD: There's this girl in my class named Nia.

DADDY: I wonder if she knows that her name is Swahili.

JAMES: Yeah she knows that girl off into all that African stuff.

MAMA: That will be enough James. The sixth day is Kummba, creativity. This is the day that we give the gifts. And the last day . . .

DADDY: Imani, faith. And I have faith that you boys can change and understand what we are trying to do.

MAMA: Now who remembers one of the days that we spoke about and what it means.

HOWARD: What's this school?

DADDY: You can learn any place son, at any time.

JESS: I can remember one, Kummba - creativity. I am a very creative person.

HOWARD: I remember Nia but I don't remember what it means.

DADDY: Purpose, we should all live our lives with purpose.

MAMA: James do you remember one?

JAMES: No.

MAMA: Well you better try.

JESS: What's next MAMA?

HOWARD: (Mimicking JESS) What's next MAMA?

MAMA: Howard you are really getting on my nerves. Next is the celebration the first day of Kwanzaa December 26. We are inviting over relatives, friends and other people we know that celebrate Kwanzaa. You know we are not the only family that is celebrating Kwanzaa.

JAMES: (In a whisper) You could have fooled me.

MAMA: Here is a book with everything in it that we have just covered why don't you look at it for a while, study it. Because we are going to do this again and when we do I expect for you to remember and know what we are talking about. Will you help me clean up Mike?

DADDY: Yeah.

(They stand and exit)

HOWARD: (To Jess) Why you always got to be Mr. Goody two shoes?

JESS: What does that mean two shoes? Every body got two shoes.

HOWARD: You know what I mean boy.

JAMES: This thing just ain't right. We didn't even get to make our own decisions we just had to this Kwanzaa thang.

HOWARD: That's right James! Go in there and tell DADDY that.

JAMES: Boy you better leave me alone.

JESS: (To James) What you gonna make for MAMA?

JAMES: I ain't gonna make her nothing.

JESS: Then what you gonna do?

JAMES: I am going to go to the store and buy every body something with the money I been saving.

JESS: You gonna get in trouble.

JAMES: No I ain't cause you ain't gonna say a word. (Walks very close to Jess.) Do you understand me?

(Jess just looks up at James and shakes his head yes.)

HOWARD: Well, man I stay in trouble I ain't going with you. I don't need no mo' trouble. I'll figure something out we got some days to go.

JESS: I kind of like this. Christmas always seemed fake to me.

HOWARD: Fake! Fake! Man I didn't hear you saying that last year when you got that new bike.

JAMES: I know that's right.

JESS: Well I'm gonna take this book and read it anybody want to join me.

HOWARD: No don't nobody want to join you.

JAMES: I see yawl later. (Yells off stage to MAMA and DADDY) I'll be back later.

(Enters Mama)

MAMA: Where you going James? Did you do your homework?

JAMES: Yeah.

MAMA: Yeah?

JAMES: Yes Mama.

MAMA: All right but you be back early.

(Exits James stage right and Mama stage left. Jess and Howard are left standing on stage looking at one another.)

HOWARD: He is going to get into some serious trouble.

JESS: Serious.

(Lights down end of Act 1 scene II)

Act 1 Scene III

(Lights come up on the home of the Bells. It is decorated in red, black, gold and green. It is the day after Christmas, the first day of Kwanzaa. Enter JAMES putting on his coat, he walks across the room as if he is going to leave the house, enters DADDY.)

DADDY: Where are you going James?

(James jumps, startled by the voice of his father.)

JAMES: Out for a few minutes DADDY.

DADDY: Out where? We need you to help out around here tonight is Umoja.

JAMES: I know Umoja, unity.

DADDY: Well, maybe you did learn something. I want you to be back in one hour.

JAMES: Yes sir.

DADDY: One hour and I mean that.

(Daddy exits. Enters Jess and Howard they are dressed in African attire. Diskis (Shirt) and Kufis (Hat).)

JAMES: Well don't you two look Af-ri-can.

JESS: You got to wear one to JAMES.

JAMES: No you see I got something to go and do.

HOWARD: What you got to do?

JAMES: Get my gift. I saw what I wanted to but the other day. Now it's gonna be on one of them day after Christmas sales and I'm gonna get it.

HOWARD: Boy you not only doing what you ain't suppose to do but you cheep to.

JESS: Yeah cheap. And you gonna get in trouble.

JAMES: When Ma' see's my gift, boy, won't be no trouble for me. See ya'.

(James exits. Daddy enters)

DADDY: Habarigani Jess? What's the news man?

JESS: I don't know nothing Daddy.

HOWARD: Yeah me either we ain't got no news.

DADDY: You suppose to say Umoja.

HOWARD: Oh, Umoja Daddy.

JESS: Yeah Umoja.

(The doorbell rings)

DADDY: I'll get that.

(Daddy walks to the door he opens it. Enters the relatives of the Bells Grandma, Grandpa, Aunts and Cousins and friends. They all hug and greet Howard, Jess and Daddy)

DADDY: Come on in everybody, we're just about ready.

(Everyone walks into the house they are laughing and talking to one anther. Enters Mama.)

MAMA: Mama, Daddy. (They hug) It's so good to see everybody. Sit down. Howard, Jess, help everyone with their coats and hats. They exit with coats and hats.)

DADDY: Habarigani!

(Everyone answers together)

Everyone: Umoja.

(They all laugh and smile and begin talking to one another as they sit waiting for the celebration to begin.)

(Enter Howard and Jess)

HOWARD: When we gonna eat I'm hungry.

MAMA: Let us first gather around the karamu table. Where is James?

HOWARD: I don't know.

Kwanzaa: A Time For Change

Just in time for the wonderful African celebration of life, harvest, and good fortunes. This play introduces children and adults to the true meaning of Kwanzaa. The main character, James, refuses to join the family's celebration of Kwanzaa and learns the difficult way that Kwanzaa is truly a beautiful family celebration.

Starring

_____*as Mama*

_____*as Daddy*

_____*as James*

_____*as Howard*

_____*as Jess*

Director _____

*Stagehands*_____

Date _____ *Time* _____

Place _____

Admit One	
Kwanzaa: A Time For Change	
Date _____ Time _____	Admit One ____
Place _____	Seat ____

Admit One	
Kwanzaa: A Time For Change	
Date _____ Time _____	Admit One ____
Place _____	Seat ____

Admit One	
Kwanzaa: A Time For Change	
Date _____ Time _____	Admit One ____
Place _____	Seat ____

Admit One	
Kwanzaa: A Time For Change	
Date _____ Time _____	Admit One ____
Place _____	Seat ____

Admit One	
Kwanzaa: A Time For Change	
Date _____ Time _____	Admit One ____
Place _____	Seat ____

Admit One	
Kwanzaa: A Time For Change	
Date _____ Time _____	Admit One ____
Place _____	Seat ____

Admit One	
Kwanzaa: A Time For Change	
Date _____ Time _____	Admit One ____
Place _____	Seat ____

Admit One	
Kwanzaa: A Time For Change	
Date _____ Time _____	Admit One ____
Place _____	Seat ____

Admit One	
Kwanzaa: A Time For Change	
Date _____ Time _____	Admit One ____
Place _____	Seat ____

Admit One	
Kwanzaa: A Time For Change	
Date _____ Time _____	Admit One ____
Place _____	Seat ____

Admit One	
Kwanzaa: A Time For Change	
Date _____ Time _____	Admit One ____
Place _____	Seat ____

Admit One	
Kwanzaa: A Time For Change	
Date _____ Time _____	Admit One ____
Place _____	Seat ____

You may photocopy or make a ticket and program like these for your
*performance of **Kwanzaa: A Time For Change***

How to Celebrate Kwanzaa

Use this section to help children understand Kwanzaa. Make copies of the following pages and pass them out to the children.

What is Kwanzaa

Kwanzaa is the African-American cultural holiday created by Dr. Maulana Ron Karenga. It begins on December 26 and ends on January 1. The word Kwanzaa comes from the African Swahili language and means "first fruit". The daily activities take place in homes, churches, or different locations in the community.

During the week of Kwanzaa, many cultural groups have different functions for each day. Go to your local bookstore, newspaper, or visit the website for information on activities in your community or neighborhood.

The Seven Symbols of Kwanzaa

On the following page are the seven symbols of Kwanzaa. The symbols or items are setup in a special place in the home or place in which the daily celebrations take place. Each symbol represent important values and principles in the African American culture.

The Seven Days of Kwanzaa

Once all the symbols (see page 109) are setup, the celebration begins The "Kinara" is the central point of the daily activities.

Each day has a special meaning by which individuals and the community plan activities. See page 110 for names, spelling, and definition of each day.

A candle lit on each day of Kwanzaa acknowledges the meaning of the day. The black candle in the center of the "Kinara" is the first candle lit. Each night following, the previous days candle is lit along with the candle that represents the meaning of the day. The lighting of the candle takes place following the meal of the day.

Through out the day, greetings are extended by saying "Habari Gani", which means, "What is the news?" The answer returned is the name of the celebration day. For example, if someone says "Habari Gani" to you on the third day, you would respond by saying "Ujima", extending your greeting in return.

The much-anticipated Kwanzaa Feast of Karumu takes place on the evening of the sixth day. This festive event is held in the community, and participates are encouraged to bring food, music, and a happy soul. This is a time for greetings, sharing thoughts and ideas, listening to speakers, and most importantly, honoring the elders.

The last day is for family gathering. After dinner, the last candle is lit and everyone discusses the meaning of each day. On the last day, family and friends exchange Zawadi (gifts).

Many African-Americans celebrate Kwanzaa regardless of religion or spiritual background. It is a wonderful tradition to teach children because of its community activities, cultural respect, and self-appreciation.

The Seven Symbols of Kwanzaa

Mkeka
A straw place mat
Symbolizes tradition and history of African Americans. All symbols are placed on Mkeka.

Kinara
A candle holder for seven candles
Symbolizes the continent of African and African ancestors. There are 3 green, 3 red, and one black candles

Mazao
Fruits and Vegatables
Symbolizes the rewards of collective labor. Place these in a bowl on the Mkeka.

Muhindi
Ears of corn.
Symbolizes the offsprings
On ear of corn should be placed on the Mkeka for each child in the family.

Kikombe Cha Umoja
Unity Cup
A cup is used to make libations in remembrance of our ancestors. It is passed around for those in attendance.

Zawadi
Gifts
Shared on the 7th day as rewards for commitments that have been kept. Usually, the gifts are handmade to avoid commercializing.

Mishumaa Saba
The seven candles that symbolize the Nguzu Saba.
3 red candles - represent blood of suffering and slavery
3 green candles - represent hope and the land of Africa
1 black candle - represent race and unity. These candles are placed in the Kinara with the red on the left, black in the center, and green on the right

Habari Gani
The Day's Greeting
Everyone extends a greeting everyday of the celebration by saying "Habari Gani", meaing "What Is The News?"
The Response
The response to the "Habari Gani" greeting is the name or meaning of the day. For example, if it's the second day, the response is "Kujichagulia, Habari Gani".

The Seven Days of Kwanzaa

1st Day
Umoja
"Unity"
To strive for and maintain unity in the family, community, nation, and race.

2nd Day
Kujichagulia
"Self-Determination"
To define, name, create opportunity, and speak for ourselves.

3rd Day
Ujima
"Collective Work"
To build, uplift, teach, and maintain our community together.

4th Day
Ujamaa
"Cooperative Economics"
To build and support our own businesses.

5th Day
Nia
"Purpose"
To define reasons and goals to collectively develop our people and communities.

6th Day
Kuumba
"Creativity"
Using our special creative talents to build economics, encourage, and teach others.

7th Day
Imani
"Faith"
To believe with all our hearts in our people, teachers, leaders, and our struggle.

Character Outline

For directors and producers to make copies, distribute, and complete with each actors in play. See "Successful Production Tips" for more information.

Name of character

What is the age of the character?

What is the character's date of birth?

Where was the character born?

What is the character's job (baker, teacher, student, lawyer, etc)?

What city does the character live in?

What time in history does the character live?

Hoes does the character walk?

How does the character talk?

Is the character tall or short, fat or thin?

Is the character married?

Does the character have any children? What ages?

Describe the personality of the character (funny, serious, like to read, athletic, etc)

Other things about the character not listed above.

Personal Information Sheet

For directors and producers to make copies, complete, and store during play rehearsal/production. See "Successful Production Tips" for more information.

Actor's Name: _____

Play Title: _____

Character: _____

Age: _____ Sex (Male/Female): _____

School: _____ Grade: _____

Home Address: _____

City: _____ State: _____ Zip: _____

Home Phone: _____ Cell Phone: _____

Fax: _____ E-mail: _____

Parent's Name: _____

About The Authors

Britt Ekland Miller began writing African American children plays after she could not find plays that were positive, uplifting, and fun. She knew that plays were a perfect way to build high self-esteem, increase confidence, and teach children how to work well with others. She also knew that in order for plays to be effective, they must closely represent the children's environment, culture, and community.

As a result, Ms. Miller has written and successfully produced many African American children plays for several organizations.

Ms. Miller is also a professional storyteller. She performs for a variety of organizations, schools, and events. She has been a featured guest on PBS's nationally acclaimed children's program "Barney and Friend's." She is also a noted poet and short story writer.

She is currently working on her new book of plays for African American children. Ms. Miller is a wife and mother of three children. She lives and works in Dallas, Texas.

Jeffery Bradley is the author of the acclaimed book entitled *"Don't Worry, Be Nappy! How To Grow Dreadlocks In America And Still Get Everything You Want.* He has written articles for various newspapers and magazines. Bradley says, "Blacks in America are unique with special talents, experiences, and knowledge. We have to share all that we know, so we can all grow together. Publishing allows me the opportunity to give back to the community what it gives me." Bradley is a husband and father of three children. He lives and works in Dallas, Texas.

Positive
African American
Plays

For Children
Book 2

➲ Fun. Easy to read with short sentences and large letters.

➲ Excellent plays for schools, churches, boys and girls clubs, programs, or anywhere children gather.

➲ Plays written by premier storyteller and playwright with several years experience working with African American Children

ISBN 1-884163-07-6
#P002 $19.95

Buffalo Soldiers

They where America's first Black soldiers who protected the West, battled in the Civil war, and fought the Indians while suffering at the hands of slavery, racism, and hate of those they protected. They are remembered through this exciting play. Children will enjoy acting out the life of the brave Buffalo Soldiers."

The Game Show

What would it feel like to be on a T.V. game show? "Tell It Like It Is" is the name of this game show. This game show is a little different – it is about African American history. Do you know your history? Be a winner and learn about famous African American and history events through this fun play.

Your Words Hurt

"Stupid," "Get out of my way," "You lazy just like your Mama", "I wished I'd never had you, my life would be much better!" Words hurt and leave scars that my never heal. In this passionate and inspirational play, children are allowed to tell how they feel about these words and try to find a solution.

Watchers

Gangs are still a threat to our children today. For many children, they are their family. In this play, children will act out the life of Phillip, a young man wanted by a gang. What will he do? Will he join or will a gang member help him to decide?

Marie, the Dancing Girl

"Stop that dancing Marie!" "You'll never be a dancer Marie", "Can't you try to do something more practical, like being a nurse?". This is a play of a young girl's dream of becoming a dancer despite the wishes of parents and teachers. With the encouragement of old Uncle Junior, Marie holds on to her dream.

Order Positive African American Plays for Children Book 2
Check with your leading bookstore or complete order form on back.

❏ YES, I want _____ copies of *Positive African American Plays for Children Book 2* at $19.95 each, plus $4 shipping per book (Texas residents pleas add $1.40 sales tax per book). Allow 15 days for delivery.

My check or money order for $ _____ is enclosed.

Please charge my ❏ Visa ❏ MasterCard

Name_____

Organization _____

Address _____

City/State/Zip _____

Phone _____ Email _____

Card # _____ Exp. Date _____

Signature_____

Please make check payable and return to:

NetNia.Com
3729 Almazan Drive
Dallas, Texas 75220

Call your credit card order to: 214-956-8346
Fax 214-956-8346, Email: netnia@netnias.com

For Faster Service Order Online
100% Secure
www.netnia.com/plays

Order Positive African American Plays for Children Book 2
Check with your leading bookstore or complete order form on back.

⊃ Fun. Easy to read with short sentences and large letters.

⊃ Excellent plays for schools, churches, boys and girls clubs, programs, or anywhere children gather.

⊃ Plays written by premier storyteller and playwright with several years experience working with African American Children

ISBN 1-884163-07-6
#P002 $19.95

Buffalo Soldiers

They where America's first Black soldiers who protected the West, battled in the Civil war, and fought the Indians while suffering at the hands of slavery, racism, and hate of those they protected. They are remembered through this exciting play. Children will enjoy acting out the life of the brave Buffalo Soldiers."

The Game Show

What would it feel like to be on a T.V. game show? "Tell It Like It Is" is the name of this game show. This game show is a little different – it is about African American history. Do you know your history? Be a winner and learn about famous African American and history events through this fun play.

Your Words Hurt

"Stupid," "Get out of my way," "You lazy just like your Mama", "I wished I'd never had you, my life would be much better!" Words hurt and leave scars that my never heal. In this passionate and inspirational play, children are allowed to tell how they feel about these words and try to find a solution.

Watchers

Gangs are still a threat to our children today. For many children, they are their family. In this play, children will act out the life of Phillip, a young man wanted by a gang. What will he do? Will he join or will a gang member help him to decide?

Marie, the Dancing Girl

"Stop that dancing Marie!" "You'll never be a dancer Marie", "Can't you try to do something more practical, like being a nurse?". This is a play of a young girl's dream of becoming a dancer despite the wishes of parents and teachers. With the encouragement of old Uncle Junior, Marie holds on to her dream.

Order Positive African American Plays for Children Book 2
Check with your leading bookstore or complete order form on back.

❑ YES, I want _____ copies of *Positive African American Plays for Children Book 2* at $19.95 each, plus $4 shipping per book (Texas residents pleas add $1.40 sales tax per book). Allow 15 days for delivery.

My check or money order for $ _____ is enclosed.

Please charge my ❑ Visa ❑ MasterCard

Name_____

Organization _____

Address _____

City/State/Zip _____

Phone _____ Email _____

Card # _____ Exp. Date _____

Signature_____

Please make check payable and return to:

NetNia.Com
3729 Almazan Drive
Dallas, Texas 75220

Call your credit card order to: 214-956-8346
Fax 214-956-8346, Email: netnia@netnias.com

For Faster Service Order Online
100% Secure
www.netnia.com/plays

How To Make Black History Month Last All Year!

Simple booklet offers great tips and ideas that help you motivate children to enjoy Black History.

Do you take for granted the importance of African American contributions to the world?

Television, radio, schools, and other forms of the media fail to highlight the wonderful contributions of Black Culture to the world.

The great Marcus Garvey once said "A people without knowledge of their history is like a tree without roots".

We owe it to the success of our children to educate and prepare them for the future by giving them the tools to succeed today.

One of the greatest gift you can give your children is knowledge about their history and culture.

This booklet will help you use your home, relatives, friends, community, and city to teach your children Black History every single day. Great ideas and tips to help you make Black History last for more than just the 28 short days of February.

Here's what this special booklet gives you: :

☑ **Compact and Easy to Read**
☑ **The Importance of Black History**
☑ **How to enjoy Black History with Your Child.**
☑ **Great Tips, Advice and Ideas**
☑ **Parents, Schools, and African American History**
☑ **Great Activities**

YES, I want to INSPIRE! my children to excellence! I've enclosed check or money order for just $7.95 Please send me "HOW TO MAKE BLACK HISTORY MONTH LAST ALL YEAR!" I understand I will also receive a free African American Parent Resource Guide:

- -

Method of Payment

☐ Check ☐ Visa ☐ MasterCard

Please make check payable and return to:
NetNia.Com, 3729 Almazan Drive
Dallas, Texas 75220
Fax 214-956-8346,
Email: netnia@netnias.com
**For Faster Service Order Online
100% Secure
www.netnia.com**

Name _____

Address _____

_____

_____

_____

Phone _____

Credit Card # _____ Exp. date _____

Signature _____

Printed in the United States
46686LVS00004BA/15

9 781884 16391